2 mínutes wíth Reality

BEJON N . DESAI

EMBASSY BOOKS
www.embassybooks.in

© Bejon N. Desai 2011

First Published in India: 2011

Published by:
EMBASSY BOOK DISTRIBUTORS
120, Great Western Building,
Maharashtra Chamber of Commerce Lane,
Fort, Mumbai-400 023, (India)
Tel : (+91-22) 22819546 / 32967415
email : info@embassybooks.in
Website: www.embassybooks.in

ISBN 13: 978-93-80227-73-3

What is Reality ?

Reality' is the 'Truth' which is perceived by the Man of honest & truthful thinking, speech and actions.

A person having the pieces as above to live the life without any hurdles of "smelly items" is "a man who honours his own voice" in within - his "Voice of CONSCIENCE".

'Reality' can come to a person enveloped in small pieces of TIME like a MOMENT. Here only one has to remain straight and one can not pull wool over his eyes. He has to embrace REALITY when it comes to get that person in her sure and secure 'embrace'.

A person who accepts this wonderful 'moment of time' can not deceive himself by any make - believe "half-truths" or "no-truths" telling the very TRUTH to slip away!..... in a disguised manner; thus proving himself not at all a MAN of TRUTH !

To make sure the reader that he is after the REALITY, the author has to lift up some REAL life situations of great people who at the point of dagger, remained stuck to 'Reality'. You will ask me a very important question and that is - "What is the difference between TRUTH and REALITY"?

'Truth' is the final stage of existence which would permit every researcher to allow the REALITY to be found and researched.

To 'Become' means to embrace EGO !
To 'Be' means to embrace REALITY !

BEJON N . DESAI

NEXT

What bewildering, demanding assignment has life given us today? What completely outrageous problem must we find a way now to solve? Whether it's leak in the plumbing, a funny noise in the car, or a raised eyebrow from our doctor, the idea of simply facing the task straightforwardly is appealing. All that is required is an open heart, a curious mind, and a willingness to engage with reality.

There are, of course, alternative ways to view the world. One of the more common approaches is to hope each morning when we open our eyes that the day will go smoothly. Smoothly being that nothing should interfere with our pre-existing plans. No unpleasant delays or detours should confront us, especially no events that make us aware of our own limitations.

If we approach life with the expectation that nothing ought to interfere with our own predilections and preferences, we are likely to resist and reject much of what happens to us. Resisting what is real, fighting with reality, getting angry and depressed with 'what is' is an exhausting and, ultimately, losing battle. Reality has a persistent way of showing up on our doorstep. We can waste a whole lot of time wishing reality were simpler, less demanding. But the ever changing circumstances of our lives keep presenting themselves to us. The critical question is: How will we respond?

We may not have the temperament or the spiritual maturity to greet every challenge with peaceful composure or to delight in whatever is God's will. It takes trust in our teachings and our Master to welcome each new disruption in our life calmly and with composure. Baba Ji has frequently reminded us that is not so important what life deals out to us as it is how we react to it.

(Spiritual Link - Sep. 2010)

It is Sheer Good Luck....

....to have good friends who help for a considerable length of time without uttering a word! Some precious names are to be mentioned in this category.

Manoj Jaikumar Tibrewala is the name I mention here with great love and gratitude. The whole family of his knows how to love us! For every act of charity and love, Manoj contributes his share without letting me know that he gives!

It seems 'giving' and 'gifting' are one and the same act for Manoj. He gets REAL pleasure and as soon as he gives he covers himself as 'the Giver'. The greatest GIVER is Lord Almighty. He gives to his loved ones - to all of us without any discrimination and remains 'in cognito' - while he gives and again gives since ages !..... this act of charity is without any noise.

Manoj has been a pillar of courage to all of us - Especially WE TWO ! Old age is compulsory and at that time some loved one does your work

which you did in your young age within no time !
He has proven to us that he has been a pillar of
strength.

My gratefulness knows no bounds -
especially when its cover is taken away and made
so bare !

This book had to pass through many
stages. In the manuscript stage i.e. the initial
stage, my writings got revised till it entered the
Computer - typing one. Manoj placed his entire
office men and machines at the disposal of this
author. He has helped me all throughout these
stages and saved me from committing lapses
and lapses to come so glaringly in the eyes of
the readers.

Even at initial, medial and final stages no
one else except Manoj could come to my succor so
graciously and well. My thanks are to him with
my blessings !

BEJON N . DESAI

Contents

Title   **Page No**

Contents

Contents

*This book is
most devotedly
dedicated*

to

Hazrat
Kamu Baba Saheb
&
Ma Hazur
Amina Banoo Saheb

BEJON

Highest & Lowest

Swami Vivekanand was on a boat going to Chicago to participate in the World's Religions' Conference. The Indian turban was attracting the attention of many people - Indians and foreigners walking or relaxing on the deck.

Swamiji was talking with most of the crowd very eager to know about his mission; as well as his services rendered to the Indian masses. Most of them were quite sincere in their enquiry.

Swami Vivekandand was very handsome and had a pair of piercing eyes. An Indian turban adorned his erudite head. He had worn English pump shoes. A man with a mischievous twinkle in his eyes asked Swamiji whether he would agree to the anomaly which was apparent in his dress, viz. Indian turban and English pump shoes.

Swamiji with a broad smile on his lips quipped - the exalted place on the body is a place of honour where the turban is and the lowest are the feet where shoes are !

Just Can Not!

Hazrat Kamu Baba, as usual, was greeting the visitors who had come to meet him and to pay respects to him in the garden of his cottage - Hira House. A very eminent Principal of a well - known residential school was almost in tears narrating to the revered Baba how badly he was treated by his boss day in and day out. How the boss shouted to him in front of others and how he had to listen to the insulting and vituperative words daily. He requested the MASTER to allow him to resign and make him free.

Baba was trying to explain to him that one has to bear the results of his "Sanchit Karmas" i.e. one's own "PRĀRABDH" and with great faith in the Lord God, one has to burn them and to make oneself free! Besides that, there is always a time to join and to resign the Institution. Lastly, whilst getting up from the bench Baba said - "Beta, the superintendent of a mad house cannot afford to be mad.

3

Whom To Invite!

"It is always very difficult to wear a smile" - when everything goes wrong. An incident from the pious life of Shri Rama proves obverse of the above statement.

Aryaputra Rama was very much above the petty trifles. The outcome of the petty minds is also very petty ! In rain or sunshine, Shri Rama was very stable.

A few days before the war with Ravana, Shri Rama with his loving friends and the followers came at a spot where the present shrine of Rameshwar is. To everyone, Shri Rama said that he felt that before going to start the war, a temple with a "Shiva-ling" be erected.

Everyone was very eager to know how it was to be done. The great "Shiva Linga" was made ready with the sand on the sea-shore! Very many helped in the process. The question was raised as to who would consecrate the Shiva

Shrine. Most of those present there were of the opinion that Shri Rama was the fittest to consecrate. Shri Rama firmly opined that Shri Ravana - the greatest devotee of Shiva be invited to consecrate the Linga!

New Home

It was evening time. The atmosphere near the sick old man's bed was sad and grim. The 86 year old grandfather had already shown his dissent for the operation that was being discussed by the two specialists who were summoned to be there to decide finally!

The grandson insisted that Dadaji must be saved; come what may! The young boy's father - the ailing man's son was quite calm and collected. He was trying to make his son understand by very many examples! The last one was very appealing! He said "A person who is trapped in a dilapidated house will have to be brought out - sooner the better ! This degenerating body cannot imprison 'Dadaji' for ever! He should now be allowed to be free. A new house (body) will welcome the 'jivatma' where he will commence his new life"! The reality touched the grandson in no small measure!

Crown Princess

An emperor and his consort were troubled and amazed at the aversion of their daughter, the crown princess, towards pomp, wealth and affluence, as well as to the sycophancy and artificiality that so often haunts the corridors of power.

From her childhood itself she was revolted by the blatant hypocrisy of the learned and the affluent of high society. As for herself, she assiduously practised self-control from pride, greed and other evils, and invariably preferred silent virtuous people to those who made a great show of their imagined virtues and piety. She was outspoken, and often lectured even religious leaders on the need of practising what they preached.

When she came of age, the emperor desired to marry her to a distinguished royal personage, but she turned down the proposition; because, she had firmly decided to marry only a "Chosen one of God". She would only agree to marry a person who bore all the qualifications of a FAKIR.

Where could the princess find such a person ? It was a very difficult task, but she herself solved the problem. She decreed that she would marry the first person who approached the city gate in the early morning of the forthcoming Friday. That person could only be a Darvesh (spiritual aspirant), returning from the desert on the outskirts of the city after attending the night-long prayer assembly (ZIKRA) in the company of his spiritual Master, a Sufi Murshad.

Sure enough, on the next Friday, a young Darvesh was the very first entrant to the city and he was brought to the palace as the chosen bridegroom. After a bath and change of dress, his NIKAH (marriage) to the Princess was immediately solemnised, and the new bride expressed her desire to move into her husband's home that very day.

Accordingly, the Darvesh brought his bride to his humble home - an abode in a desolate place. It was a dilapidated hut.

She boldly went in. Save for a torn prayer -

8

carpet and two empty vessels, there was nothing else inside. In the cornice of the thatched hut wall, there were two mouldy pieces of bread (naan). She indignantly asked why those pieces were there at all! The Darvesh replied that they were kept in reserve in case, there was nothing else to eat!

The Princess was very annoyed at this and she and her husband part immediately. The Darvesh expressed equal annoyance at the Princess's pampered attitudes. If two pieces of bread were the reason for her displeasure, he too would prefer separation!... he asserted.

But the Princess shot back: 'You show to the world that you are a Darvesh, but you are not! Your long Fakir's robe does not fit your behaviour. If you are really a Fakir, where is the need to keep two pieces of bread handy, just in case you needed them! Is this what you call your total dependence on the Lord? You should either accept the fact of you hypocrisy, or you should immediately throw away these two pieces of dried bread.

Even under the crushing REALITY of abject poverty, the royal Princess spoke thus. She it was who was later known as Saint Raabia.

Masterji - M

Swami Ramkrishna Paramhansji was suffering from Carcinoma of the tongue, which was spreaded to his throat also. Very many disciples and lovers of Swamiji made it a routine to stand near his sick bed and request Swamiji to speak less with visitors who came in large numbers daily to meet the MASTER.

There was an ardent devotee who was affectionately known as 'Masterji' who, later, wrote Shri Ramkrishnaji's biography under the pen name of 'M'. His name was Mahendranath Gupta and he was the Headmaster of a School in Calcutta. He loved to call himself 'M'. He faithfully recorded the conversations of the great master a century ago. He was standing near the ailing Master and beseeched him to fix his mind on the diseased parts i.e. his tongue and the throat. Ramkrishnaji smilingly asked him whether he should withdraw his mind that was already dedicated to PARAM-ĀTMA and fix it on the decaying parts of his body. Would it be proper to do so?

Death is Compulsory

DEATH is inevitable. It is unavoidable. It is very essential. It is with us since our beginning. Each breath is hurling us little by little towards death. Imagine a state of deathlessness in this world. Think of bees, birds, animals and human beings living for thousands of years on end!

Can you imagine the state of a world full of old, ailing and bed - ridden people in trillions doing nothing else besides awaiting the Lord's order for a change from a state of immortality to a state of death ! At a juncture like this, human beings themselves would ask the lord to make them mortal.

A breath that is inhaled is the breath of life and a breath that is exhaled is the breath of death - and when it comes in again, it is life and again when it goes out, it is death. Thus every minute do we live and every minute do we die! We have to be alert therefore and do not be oblivious of our hereafter.

Death Doesn't Destroy

Soul is immortal; but this body too does not die! The matter contained in the body gets disbursed and distributed in five parts after the passing away of the CHAITANYA (energy force) from the body and that phenomenon is called DEATH.

The body is made up of FIVE ELEMENTS (Anasars) or PANCHA MAHABHUTA. They are:

i)   **WATER :** 75 per cent of our body -weight is WATER in the form of liquid - like Serum, blood, urine, and so on.

ii)   **EARTH :** flesh, muscles, sinews, bones and solid parts of the body external as well as internal.

iii)   **FIRE** : the heat and energy which maintains the normal temperature of the body at 98.05 degrees and continuously sustains this frame, as also the VAISHWANARA - the VISHNU - FIRE, that keeps awake our hunger and appetite and sustains all life.

iv) **AIR** : the wind element Prana, Apana, Vyana, Udana, and so on.

v) **SPACE** : Avakasha - from where we draw all our imagination, laughter, sorrow, intuition and intangible faculties.

At the time of human conception, all these are provided through the confluence of semen and ovum, along with the genes and chromosomes that are inherent in the "CLOT" (as indicated in the Koran - i - Sharif) that gradually and surely develops into a human body after nine months of preservation. When the foetus in the womb is made, all the five elements vigorously combine to give it shape, form and weight through their five components - "Panchabhuta" - of earth, water, fire, air and space. They work inside the womb after it.

All these five elements are dynamic and help the human body to grow before as well as after birth. The atman (soul) acts only as a witness; because, it is already a fully developed entity that remains as it is from the time of birth to death.

When the so called "end" comes, each "Mahabhuta" - great elemental entity in nature takes back its own estate and property and that too with interest. Water merges into water; and in the same way, air, earth, fire and space merge into their elemental entities. New things start growing in the earth, nourished by the same water, air, fire and space. They are imbibed and enjoyed by COUPLES - men and women; and once again children are born to them, the continuity of life remaining unbroken!

This beautiful earth receives by way of death and gives all these five elements back by way of birth and creation.

Where is death ? Where is the end? It is not an end! Does even matter die?   It is mere transformation! ISN'T LIFE DEATHLESS? That is the REALITY.

'My Cap' - means 'Meri Topi'

In the days of yore in India, 'English' language was taught and learnt through (PĀTHMĀLĀ) - small books especially written in regional languages by reverend priests of Christianity. One such book written by Rev. Taylor contained Lesson No. 3 with the caption of the Lesson named "My CAP".

In a small village in a primary school, the 3rd Std. teacher wrote "My CAP" on the board. Down below the words My CAP, Guruji wrote its meaning in vernacular : MERI TOPI. All the youngsters copied the same in their exercise books. Only one student wrote My CAP; but didn't write MERI TOPI; because Guruji had written 'MY CAP' and 'MERI TOPI'. He, therefore, wrote in his book "My Cap" - meaning "GURUJI KI TOPI" because it was Guruji who wrote 'My CAP' meaning "MERI TOPI" and the little one rightly thought it was his (Guruji's)

Topi. He went home and started doing home-work orally.

This youngster was the product of a middle class home. His father had just returned from his work-place and had reclined in an easy-chair. His mother was preparing tea in the Kitchen.

The boy was loudly uttering 'My CAP' - means 'GURUJI KI TOPI'. The father listened to these utterances for some time and asked his son loudly not to say 'GURUJI KI TOPI'; but asked him to say the correct meaning : 'My CAP' means 'MERI TOPI'. The boy, being shouted down, didn't say a word in front of his father; but quietly wrote in his book 'MY CAP' at School means 'Guruji ki Topi' and at home, it is PITAJI KI TOPI' - (father's cap).

Next day was the day of inspection. The inspector entered the class and enquired regarding the lesson going on in the class. After ascertaining from the teacher, he wrote on the board 'My CAP' and looked at all the learners in the class. That one youngster - who looked very nervous - was made to stand up and reply. The boy facing the REALITY - said in a hesitating manner that My CAP, whilst in school, means Guruji Ki Topi i.e. Teacher's cap and My CAP - in the home, means Father's cap - PITAJI KI TOPI.

The Inspector got very angry, scolded the teacher and informed the very nervous pupil that My CAP is neither 'Teacher's Cap' nor 'Father's Cap; but it means : 'My CAP'.

The boy wrote in his book 'My CAP' means 'INSPECTOR KI TOPI' on an Inspection Day!

Silence

"Silence is a state of the consciousness which comes of itself from above when you open to the Divine Consciousness.

Silence is the condition of the being when it returns to the Divine.

Silence is a state in which either there is no movement of the mind or vital or else a great stillness which no surface movement can pierce or alter.

Silence is the absence of all motion of thought or other vibration of activity. "

Sri Aurobindo

Get to What Is !

"Can we not be aware of everything AS IT IS !
To get to what IS, is the end of the struggle.
To BE AWARE, to know what ONE IS, is the
beginning of wisdom.
We can have understanding of what is, only
when we recognise it without
Condemnation, Justification or
Identification.
We must begin to understand ourselves.
We must know ourselves as we ARE.
Not as we wish to be.
The understanding of oneself is seeing onself
from moment to moment in the mirror of
relationships to property, to things, to people
and to ideas. "

J. Krishnamurti

The New Year

"
The years roll on, but we are far from home.
May each day of the new year take us
at least one step closer to the Mother
Divine.

Every night, as we retire, may the
prayer be on our lips : "Nearer Ma, to Thee!
I seek your blessings in the ONE SERVICE. "

(Dada) J. P. Vaswani

Says Sahajo

"
Even success in the world
without the Guru is not possible
Much less will soul meet the Lord
without the help of Guru "

Sahajoba

20

66

Consciousness incarnates into the manifested dimension, that is to say, it becomes form. When it does so, it enters a dreamlike state. Intelligence remains, but consciousness becomes unconscious of itself.
It loses itself in form, becomes identified with forms. This could be described as the descent of the divine into matter. 99

Eckhart Tolle

66

The intellectual knows not the path,
And yet he proudly broadcasts his wise folly.
His Self and Supreme Self are within him,
But the poor fellow always searches eagerly outside. 99

Kabir

Stand Apart and Yet Support!

Khalil Gibran was a mystic of the very highest order. There was a time when this mystic was not at all accepted by the people. He was excommunicated from his own country. Again, the time came when he was so very much acclaimed by those who slighted him that he was buried near the same place of worship from where he was routed and hooted out! Some of his best works are: "Spirit Rebellious"; "The Prophet"; "The Garden of Prophet"; "Jesus, the Son of Man"; "Gardener".

His beloved Barbara Young was, no doubt, drawn very much to Khalil and yet she was admonished to keep a respectable distance from the love that can not endure! He says, "Let there be spaces in your togetherness"; "Fill each other cup: but drink not from one cup"!; "Give one another of your bread; but eat not from the same loaf"; "And stand together yet not too near together". He gives the reason for these sayings! "For the pillars of the temple stand apart".

So Much For A Whistle!

The great literary scholar of prose Benjamin Franklin's masterpiece "How much for your whistle?" is referred to by me here.

When he was a child of seven years old, his friends, on a holiday filled his pockets with coppers; he went directly to a shop where all sorts of toys were available. Franklin was charmed with the sound of a whistle that was blown by a boy on the road. He resolved to have that whistle from him at any cost; and so voluntarily he, being a child, offered and gave all his money for a whistle! He came home and went on whistling and disturbing the whole family.

All the members of the family laughed at him very much for his folly of paying such large amount for a whistle! All this gave him more chagrin than the whistle gave him pleasure. When he grew old and when he was tempted to buy something not necessary, he said to himself 'don't give too much for the whistle'; and he saved money.

Aren't we doing the same thing to our precious life? So grown-up in body we are; but so childish we are in mind! We buy junk and trinkets, paying very heavy prices at times!

Most of the ills and evils of our society are due to "giving too much for the whistle"! Liquor, tobacco, drugs, gambling and similar such vices take a toll of our good and fruitful life!

Foolish thoughts, words and acts of a human being bring him untold misery and make his life utterly wretched in body, mind and spirit! We must not pay so much for a whistle!

For Twenty Long Years!!

In the Province of Isphahan, a very well - known Darvesh took a solemn vow to pray at all the five watches of the day, as well as to conduct DHIKRA (the constant remembering of the name/s of God) right through the night.

He offered his prayers sitting at one fixed place in a corner of a Masjid (mosque). Every day after his evening prayers, he addressed the Lord loudly, thus; "O my Lord! Thou alone art the light of my eyes and the flower of my speech. Thou alone art my support and strength, and I turn for supplication to none except Thee! I do not desire any wealth, because Thou alone art all my wealth; and without Thee, I would be the poorest of all creatures! I do not pray to get anything from Thee except for one thing - your Deedar - a Vision of Thee! Fulfill this desire of mine, O my Lord, and I shall never ask anything else from Thee!"

He prayed incessantly in this manner

every day after his evening prayers for almost twenty years. Just one more day remained for a span of full twenty years to come to an end. Those who prayed with him in the mosque were expecting a KARISHMA, a miracle, with full confidence. They had known and revered the Darvesh, who always prayed on bended knees at a fixed place in the mosque, for all these many years. Two concave dents, carved into the floor by the weight of his knees, gave silent proof of his intense devotion and marathon endurance.

It was now the last day of his twentieth year of incessant worship and veneration, but the whole day passed most uneventfully to the disappointment of the gathered people who were expecting a miracle without understanding the silent play of Providence. As soon as the evening (Maghreb) Namaz congregation was about to disperse, the Darvesh, oblivious of the Lord's inaction to show a miracle, prepared to start his usual supplication. Just then, a thunderous vibration, filling the entire firmament, was suddenly heard by everyone down on earth. It was a revelation from the UNKNOWN up above at last!

People heaved a sigh of relief, with the joy in their hearts imprinted on their faces. The mighty noise suddenly metamorphosed into a booming voice. A revelation! It proclaimed : "Know ye, O Darvesh, thy prayers have not been accepted by the Lord!" The voice faded back to where it had come from. There was a hush at first, and then a confused murmuring. Twenty years of penance.... and this reward!

But the Darvesh, who was in a sort of trance after the divine proclamation, suddenly got up and started dancing in dizzy whirls, as if expressing his gratefulness to the Lord for his precious favour. People asked him why he was dancing with such joy when his prayers were not accepted. He, in great ecstasy, replied, "Who cares for the acceptance! I am overjoyed that the Lord HEARD my prayers and talked with me! What more can I expect from the Lord"?

Who Am I ?

It was a question - answer hour. Mātāji Anandmoyi Mā was giving answers to the questions asked by the devotees in the morning session of the Sanyam (संयम) Saptah (सप्ताह).

The question asked was : "WHO AM I?" The first person singular Pronoun 'I' was coming 1st in the series of PERSONAL PRONOUNS. Mātāji opened my eyes. She said, "Lāl, 'I' is the word which does not stay longer with any one as soon as another person starts talking!" That other person will address in a magic way and the pronoun 'I' will turn into 'YOU' and that has to be accepted!.... because it is so true! The person speaking uses I and all of a sudden, he will be addressed as YOU by the person who speaks with you! Again this 'You' will be changed into HE as soon as he talks with someone in your absence! This is what everyone's I is! It has no longevity or any sort of stability or permanence!

Cantos and Liberation

The founder of the Swaminarayan Cult Shri Sahajanand Swami was bringing great awakening through his discourses. Those who were not even mediocre in morals or upon any mark at any level started understanding Swamiji's message contained in his discourses.

At that time, a great Sanskrit Scholar named Shri Dinanath Bhatt came to meet Swamiji. He was a great Sanskrit Pandit of that time. It was futile to compete with Panditji in Sanskrit Grammar and Prosody (Pingal).

Swamiji welcomed this great learned Pandit and complimented him by saying, "You are by far a great learned scholar of Sanskrit. Your learning is praised by every one in Society; Tell me, Panditji, how many shlokas (cantos) are on the tip of your tongue?" Panditji thought that Swamiji was testing him.

To this question of Swamiji, Pandit Dinanath replied, "In all, eighteen thousand! If it is desired, Panditji was ready there and then for the recital of all the cantos. To which Swamiji again asked "Tell me, Dinanathji, how many out of these Shlokas will be of use to you in acquiring MOKSHA - Salvation?"

Panditji slipped into silence for quite some time and then expressed his regrets by saying that he had never ever thought of achieving any salvation through the help of some of these cantos.

Panditji bowed in submission and added that it was an expression of the enormity of his knowledge and yet he was groping in the dark regarding using his enormous knowledge in acquiring salvation in life.

The Truth was made apparent by Sahajanand Swami to Pandit Dinanath.

Swami - Means A Master

It was a serious throat ailment from which Shri Ramkrishna Paramhansji was suffering. A couple of (so-called) disciples were spreading a rumour that this ailment was due to Shri Ramkrishna partaking 'PRASAD' which was known as BHOG - a sacrificial offering every day placed before the DEVI. This rumour came to the ears of Swamiji. He smiled and commented that the Prasad is to be taken as an offering to the deity in a very negligible proportion with great reverence. It is not to be consumed as food!

One evening, Swamiji saw in the crowd gathered around him those two who were spreading this story. He asked them to bring some "Castor Sugar" (PITHI SAKAR i.e. finely crushed sugar powder). On its arrival Swamiji asked one of his near disciples to place a tea-spoon full of it on his tongue and summoned him to blow off the powder from his tongue after full 60 seconds, i.e. one full minute. This finely crushed sugar powder will melt immediately within two seconds after it is placed on the tongue.

As per Swamiji's instruction, the crushed sugar powder was blown off by the disciple after a minute. There was neither a trace of his saliva nor the powder. The tongue was totally dry! Thereby Swamiji proved that whatsoever he was having through his tongue was devoid of any taste or any pleasure born out of senses!

Ocean of Knowledge

The great social reformer, educationist and the well renowned writer Ishwarchandra was given an honourable title of VIDYĀSĀGAR. He established schools for girls. He advocated to impart education to widows who were barred from all such activities at that time. To set an example, he married his son to a widow only. Queen Victoria of England honoured him with the then most coveted title of C.I.E.

He was invited by very many foreign Institutions of learning to deliver lectures there. Once under the chairmanship of Vidyāsāgar, a seminar was arranged when he was in England. He was a stickler of time and therefore he went to the place on the dot; and to his surprise he found that the organisers of the function were standing in small groups and discussing something seriously. Ishwarchandra found out that the Janitor staff (cleaners) had not come that day and the place had remained uncleaned!

Ishwarchandra quipped - "even if the janitors could not make it, it is alright! But we are there! Let us start!" So saying he himself started cleaning the place! Lo and behold! The place was cleaned five minutes before the scheduled time!

Cleaning is a good work! The Lord is always pleased to see the human beings doing good work!

Can Bullets be Turned into Chocolates ?

Poet Sundaram from Pondicherry, was in my Institution - staying with my School Vice Principal Rasik Shah. His Sojourn was a blessing to all of us! He had come for the immersion of his wife's 'asthi' after her passing away!

A day prior to his return, he agreed to address our School Assembly. He preferred to speak in the 'open forum'. The students asked quite a few intelligent questions. The last question by a middle school section inmate was this: "Gandhiji had proved to the people through his spiritual practices that he was a great soul - a MAHĀTMĀ! Why, then, he could not perform a miracle ? Why had he to die because he was shot?" Sundaram was pleased to get a question of this sort! He said: "If water can not soak; or fire can not burn; or the wind can not dry up - it would be termed as unnatural and untrue! Fire has to burn; water has to soak and wind has to make something dry! That's   TRUTH   and that is universally accepted!

"Gandhiji, in his entire life time, accepted TRUTH like one's own breath! Therefore he accepted a bullet as an instrument of killing - that was   TRUTH! Thus, bullets could not be turned into chocolates! That would have been totally an UNTRUTH!"

Power and Wisdom

Material affluence and spiritual prowess are both POWERS. A rich person who is bereft of right - mindedness will either waste his wealth or turn out to be a despot. A spiritual person bereft of sufficient means will go into oblivion. Both are powers; and both are to be tamed and used in the right way. The life of King Ibrahim teaches us the lesson not to be superficially pious on the strength of the power of money and influence.

King Ibrahim's vast kingdom and great affluence had no bounds. Inwardly, his ego was much puffed up with his power, pomposity and prosperity. But outwardly, he wanted to show to the world that he was very Saintly and Charitable, despite his riches and power. So he publicly gave alms on the streets of his capital city, and loved to hear people praising his goodness. His courtiers who knew him only too well, took full advantage of his superficial piety. Thus, King Ibrahim had more flatterers than friends. They flattered him so much about his prayerful life, that he actually came to believe in his saintly status.

Within a short time, the King became a megalomaniac. He grew to consider himself a highly realised soul, and regularly invited sages and philosophers to his court. He built himself a seven - storeyed minar (representing the seven heavens) for his prayers, which he offered from a room on the top floor, in full view of the populace. He would pray very loudly so that all may hear him, but he kept guards in four shifts of six hours each to prevent anyone from entering the private minar.

One day, the king was praying as loudly as ever, when he heard someone knocking at the prayer - room door. At first, he ignored the sound and continued with his prayers. But then the knocking turned into a banging which drowned even the King's prayers. King Ibrahim angrily opened the door to find a Fakir (mendicant) who asked the king: "I have lost my camel! Has it come here ?" The Fakir asked this question in the most placid manner.

King Ibrahim's wrath knew no bounds! He asked the Fakir how he had been allowed to come up to the seventh floor. And besides, how could a camel even climb seven floors? To this the mendicant meekly replied that he too was perplexed, but only at the King's mode of prayer.

"Does the King believe that his loud prayers reach The Lord faster because they are offered from the seventh floor? A camel can't climb seven storeys, and neither can your prayers reach the seventh heaven!" So saying, the mendicant climbed down the stairs and disappeared into thin air.

The King went in search of the Fakir, but he could not find him anywhere. BUT that encounter changed his life! He became self - realised. He thirsted for REAL spirituality. He quickly gathered his courtiers as well as his family members, and there and then announced that up till now, he was very far away from the REALITY and that he was NOW immediately renouncing his position and all that went with it.

For the rest of his life, he wandered from clime to clime and all over the earth, barefooted and acquired REAL spiritual prowess after very many years. He was later known as SAINT IBRAHIM.

Revile Not Dust !

" Farid, revile not dust,
　　　　　there is nothing like it.
When we are alive,
　　　　　it is beneath our feet.
When we are dead,
　　　　　It is above us. "

Baba Farid

Not A Jot !

" To fate surrender
　　　　with good grace;
Resigned accept it
　　　　less or more;
Whatever the PEN has writ
　　　　the SCORE
No Jot thereof shall it efface. "

Omar Khayyam

Sunder Says

66

The perfect Master showered his grace
upon me, and showed me God !
...... so close to me !
       Why are you wandering about
uselessly?
If you wish to find God, go to the Guru. 99

Sahajoba

Love

66

Love cannot exist under the pressure,
tension and dissension caused by doubt
and suspicion.

   Love's existence is impossible
under such conditions. It is like water
& oil, which repel one another these
two can never mix. 99

Kamu Baba

41

Freeze it

"

Freeze the water and it will be turned into ice. Water was in its liquid stage : Any pebble thrown into the liquid will create whirls. The whirls will stop if the water is turned into ice. Freezing the water, it will certainly create ice and ice will not respond, if any pebble is thrown into it; because ice cannot create whirls when anything is thrown into it; because it has lost its capacity to create whirls.

Freeze the liquidity of the mind and the mind will lose its liquidity. No whirls when pebbles of slight and insult are thrown; because it is frozen and has lost its ability to respond as whirls.

This is the sure way to overcome the feelings of slights and insults. "

("The Master")

42

Good Deeds

"
To gain the reward of good deeds and to win forgiveness for my misdeeds,
I perform righteous acts for the love of my soul;
All the good deeds of all the good people
Throughout the seven spheres,
Shall get their share of blessings
As wide as the earth;
As extensive as the river;
As exalted as the sun;
May you be righteous and long lived.
May it come about as I entreat.

Righteousness is the best gift of God.
It is bliss (inner happiness).
Happiness is unto him who is righteous
For the sake of achieving further righteousness. "

Zorastrian Scripture :
KERFEH MOZD & ASHEM VOHU

Humble and Yet Apt

Gandhiji was to go to Orissa one day and therefore he was standing on the platform with some of his coworkers, waiting for the train.

At that very time, a very poor person from the tribal area approached Bapu and prostrated in utter gratitude mumbling words of thankfulness to Gandhiji. Bapu made him stand up near him and at that time that half-naked tribal offered one paisa to Gandhiji with utter reverence! Gandhiji, getting amazed, asked him as to why he did so!

The poor man expressed his great gratitude towards Bapu and said, "As and when we go to Mandir - we bow down to the deity and place an offering that we could afford!

"You are our living God (Deva) and therefore you deserve all our respect by way of prostration as well as our humble offering! Please accept the same and oblige".

"You are More Learned!"

Once, it so happened that Swami Ramatirthaji went for an early morning bath in Prayag near a place of scenic beauty called Ram Baug. Pandit Malaviyaji and Bhikshu Akhandanandji were also with him.

After the bath, Swami Ramatirthaji reached the Ganga River Bank. Akhandanandji was holding his "KAUPIN" (Change Cloth) and was waiting for Ramatirthaji to come out of the river.

Both Malaviyaji and Akhandanandji saw Swamiji's feet laden with mud galore! The reaction from Malaviyaji was instantaneous. He did not wait for a moment and bringing out his precious scarf (Khes) started cleaning the mud from Ramatirthaji's feet! Swamiji's sudden reaction was one of "shock" and in a humble tone Swamiji told Malaviyaji that such a precious scarf should not have been soiled! After all Malaviyaji was more learned than him!.

Immediately replied Malaviyaji that one who has renounced everything was more worthy of adoration and honour than one who has been gathering Knowledge!

"Cease to Become a Fool!"

It was the end of Siddharth's great princely search of TRUTH. His followers were sitting outside the Jataka Grove wherein he was meditating. It was the 40th day of his inner search.

He came out with an unexplainable radiance on his face. His smile was not of this earth! His followers Panchkauri and Anand were pleasantly asking some questions! Anand said, "Master! You seem to be very happy! Why?" The Prince replied, "Yes, I am happy because I am Buddha today". Panchkauri asked, "Can you give us further reason for your happiness?" Buddha said, "I am happy because I have ceased to become a fool!.... from today! I am now and shall always remain an enlightened one i.e. Buddha!"

"Has it not been a REALITY that we are afraid of REALITY? We feel nothing even when we embrace UNTRUTH!"

The next day, Buddha - The Master elaborated upon what he had said the previous day.

Buddha said, "After much pondering and continuous meditation, I came to some very important conclusions :

i)   By starving the mind, nothing will be achieved! By starving the body, the capacity to think clearly will be lost! These are the STARK REALITIES!

ii)   The middle PATH of 'Moderation' will be of great benefit. That path has led me to four truths.

iii) These 4 truths are:

1)   Pain is! (That means "There is Pain").

2)   There is cause of Pain.

3)   There is cessation of Pain.

4)   There is remedy to be free from it and that is NIRVĀNA and that is through VIPASSANĀ -meditation wherein one has to give some work to one's own MIND and OBSERVE blankly! See in within!

A Dacoit Named Vāliā

Vāliā epitomised wickedness, murder, dacoity and all the evil that goes with such deeds. One day he stopped an ascetic on the highway and threatened him with death if he did not hand over whatever be had in his possession. The ascetic told him that he had renounced the world, and therefore to find any worldly wealth upon his person was an impossibility!.

That retort angered Vāliā very much. He would have empty hands on that day too, because on all previous three days he had met nobody on the road who could be looted.

The ascetic tried hard to persuade him to desist from all atrocities. Vāliā, in his wrath and temper, told him that killing a person or plundering a passerby was nothing heinous for him, because he was most displeased with Providence. His destiny had treated him most cruelly! The ascetic asked him why he had taken to the evil way of life. Vāliā replied that he knew no other way; for, he was averse to working hard to earn a normal living by the sweat of his brow. Besides, he had so many mouths to feed at home that his frustration knew no bounds.

The ascetic said that he was prepared to die at Vāliā's hands, provided that Vāliā first went home and enquired from his family members whether they agreed to share the responsibility of the evil and atrocious acts that he habitually committed! Vāliā was hesitant to leave the ascetic alone; but upon the righteous assurance of the ascetic, he left for his home.

Vāliā asked his parents, his wife and all the young and old members of his family whether they agreed to share responsibility for whatever he did to bring money home. Everyone told him that it was his duty to support them in any way he chose. They were, they said, in no way connected with whatever he did to earn! It was he alone who was responsible for whatever acts he performed to maintain his home and family.

Vāliā was stunned. He returned to the ascetic and touched his feet, saying : "Oh Wise One! You have opened my eyes. You have shown me that the punishment for my bad deeds will be mine alone! Hence, from this day forth I too shall renounce my wicked ways; It is too great a burden for me to bear alone!

Baba Farid & Jilebis

Baba Farid a sufi saint of great repute attracted large crowds of devotees every day. Once every week a poor young widow labourer used to attend his assembly. One day, she got up early, and after her bath, prayers and other daily chores, mended the tattered clothes of her only son and washed them. Once they were dry, she folded and pressed them heavily with her hands. Later, after bathing her son, she opened her purse and counted her savings : eleven annas in all! Since she was working as a lowly menial labourer, this paltry sum represented a full month's savings!

The next day was her son's birthday, so after his bath she applied 'itra' (flower - extract) on him. Her son on that day looked like a Prince to her, and she asked him to accompany her to the bazar where she purchased one seer of 'jilebi' (Indian sweets) worth eight annas and two 'itra fāhyās' (cotton buds) which cost her an anna. Now, all she had left was a mere two annas. With the child, she reached the Zāviā (abode) of Baba Farid, prostrated herself before him.

She said, "Baba, I am a very poor labourer but a special occasion today demands your blessings for my son. It happens to be his birthday. So saying, she applied 'itra' to Baba Farid and placed before him the packet of Jilebis that she had brought. Baba Farid prevented her from opening it as if declining her gift. She was greatly shocked and taken aback due to this gesture! In the meantime, Baba called her son before him and began chanting 'duās' (blessings). While doing so, he looked lost in reverie, as if he was physically there but spiritually elsewhere! Tears flowed freely down his cheeks. Gradually, he opened his eyes, asked for the packet of Jilebis and opened it himself. After distributing them to everyone around him, he put a piece or two into the mouths of the mother and the son.

Then, lo and behold! he started devouring all the remaining pieces with such gusto that within a minute, the packet contained nothing!

The mother's eyes filled with tears. She exclaimed, "Baba, I shall never forget this great blessing bestowed on us today, but...! "Baba, why did you refuse my gifts at the start?"

The saint softly murmured, "today was my day of fasting and that is the only reason why I behaved in that uncouth manner but just then, I heard this thundering admonition from God" : "Farid, in observing your fast today, will you hurt this poor widow who offered almost entire wealth to you in the form of these sweets? Do such occasions come your way every day? Pray do not hurt her feelings! You are hurting me by hurting her!"

No-Mind State

As far as possible, one will have to evolve a method by which one can give some work to the MIND! Seers and Saints of yore kept their mind occupied in 'REMEMBRANCING' (mentally taking) the Lord's name continuously. Sufis called it 'ZIKRA' (DHIKRA). Indian Saints called it BHAKTI - Nama Smarana.

Why did they give such work to the mind? Because, they observed that the mind has the habit of slipping in the Murky Past or the Murky Future!

When the mind slips into the murky Past, it becomes angry.

E.g. So and so insult__ed__ me! So and so abus__ed__ me! See the Past Tense used in the Verb.
OR
I __will__ __show__ him his place! I __will__ __kill__ him. The future tense is underlined in both these sentences.

As the murky Past draws one into anger, so the murky Future draws one into false pride. So, what is the solution to keep away ourselves from anger & pride?

ACT IN THE IMMEDIATE PRESENT!
THAT   IS   REALITY!

Position and Disposition

A very robust man developed cataracts in both his eyes. After some time, the doctor inspected his eyes and thought that an operation in the right eye was imperative. So, a date was decided for the purpose. In the meanwhile, the eye surgeon heard a faint voice, along with quiet but insolent laughter. Both were emanating from the cataract of the right eye.

The cataract was vaingloriously bragging to the doctor how powerful it was, and how it had succeeded in making such a strong man helpless! The surgeon merely smiled and went away.

On the appointed day, the operation was performed, and the limp little cataract was extracted and held in the pincers. The surgeon then addressed it thus: "You - an insignificant tiny speck of matter - did not make this able bodied man helpless. It was not you at all!!! It was only the place in which you somehow happened to be sitting that was so critical. Today, you are out and dethroned, and your new place now will be in the gutter! Let's see how powerful you find yourself in your new seat!"

The Shepherd's Prayer

Moses saw a Shepherd on the way crying : "O Lord! who choosest Thou to sew Thy shoon and comb Thy hair? That I may wash Thy clothes? Kill Thy lice and bring milk to Thee? O Worshipful one! That I may kiss Thy little hand and rub Thy little feet and sweep Thy little room at bed time?"

On hearing these foolish words, Moses said, "Man, to whom are you speaking? What babble! What blasphemy and raving! Stuff some cotton into your mouth! Truly, the friendship of a fool is enmity to the High God who is not in want of such like service."

The shepherd rent his garment, heaved a sigh; and took his way to wilderness.

Then came to Moses a Revelation:

"Thou hast parted My servant from Me. Were you sent as a prophet to unite or wert thou sent to severe? I have bestowed on everyone a particular mode of worship. I have given everyone a peculiar form of expression. By hurting my lover you have hurted Me! You insulted My servant by degrading him!"

The divine Revelation continued:

"The idiom of Hindustan is excellent for Hindus; The idiom of Sind is excellent for the people of Sind. I look NOT at tongue and speech; I look at the spirit and the inward feeling!

"I look into the heart to see whether it be lowly, though the words uttered be not lowly! Enough of phrases and conceits and metaphors! I want burning!... burning!

Light up a fire of LOVE in thy soul; burn away all thought and expression!

"O Moses! They that know the conventions are of one sort, they whose souls burn are of another!"

"The religion of love is apart from all religions. The lovers of God have no religion but God alone! They love God and God alone is their religion."

Taking Good Care of the Material Things

Mataji at the International School at Pondicherry was answering the question placed by a foreign student. He wondered why one should be so materially conscious, when one's goal in life is only to search for the Divine in its purest form. He was of the opinion that it was a sheer waste of time to take care of insignificant material objects like pens, etc. when the lofty goal is to reach the Divine itself!

Mataji gave him a fitting reply. She asked him to give her his pen. It happened to be a 'Parker', the finest make of pen; leak - proof, rust - proof, perfectly balanced etc. She asked the young aspirant to imagine the technical processes and care required for the manufacture of such a precision instrument. The student agreed that careful planning and design, sophisticated machines, trained staff, the best of materials of a high standard must have gone into its production. Then, Mataji asked a very simple question: 'Son, tell me, who must have given the inspiration to the manufacturers to conceive and produce this material object in all its perfection?' The boy replied with great delight, "Oh yes, Mother, it is only the Divine that inspires everything!" Mataji finally said, "Then, if you misuse any material object inspired by the Divine, don't you think that you are also insulting the Divine itself?"

Two Eternal Questions

A true aspirant is very anxious to know what necessity there was for offering prayers when every event in a person's life occurs in a pre-planned and predestined manner by Providence. If events are to occur with an absolute certainty in a person's life, how could prayers make an inch of difference.

The Second question was a logical corollary to the first. If prayers had no power to change the pre-destined course of events, in what sense could they be said to protect a person from the sufferings that were inexorably due to rain upon him?

Let us answer these two questions in the same order in which they are asked. First, about the necessity of PRAYERS. Prayer in Persian is called IBĀDAT for BANDAGI (Service). In Sanskrit, it is known as PRĀRTHANĀ or ARCHANĀ (Supplication). The Lord knows our needs and necessities much before they are placed before the Lord in the form of prayers. It is also true that under the immutable divine law, all the joys and sufferings that come to a person are pre-determined.

Happiness and suffering come either in singles or number. Suppose Mr. X is to receive a fifty-ton load of suffering. Now, with prayers, the fifty tons will not be lessened - not a bit will be assuaged. But it could be better distributed, a little, a bit by bit at a time - say a small load of two tons only, on twenty five different occasions. Therefore, the Lord God is called RAHMĀN-HIR-RAHIM i.e. the Just and the Merciful. It is not possible to acquaint someone as JUST as well as the MERCIFUL. Either one is only JUST or only MERCIFUL. One can not administer JUSTICE as well as MERCY both. Ordinarily, one finds it difficult to administer both MERCY and JUSTICE at the same time. And yet in administering the preordained load of 50 tons, the Lord God is JUST and whilst administering the load he does it distributing it twenty five times in small proportions of twentyfive times - both simultaneously without delay or error!

Now about the second question. The answer to the first question just needs to be slightly elaborated.

"ZINDAGI BARĀE BANDAGIST
ZINDAGI BIN BANDAGI; SHARMINDAGIST"

This is Persian couplet.
It says : The life is for PRAYERS.
The life without PRAYERS is a SORROW (Or SHAME).

Prayer is like an umbrella (PARASOL). By opening an umbrella and holding it over your head, you do not stop rain or heat from descending from above; but you surely protect yourself from the direct blasts of both - i.e. rain and heat!
Prayer neither can stop rain nor also can stop heat!.... like an umbrella; but the umbrella can PROTECT you from BOTH - Rain and Heat. Everything will you; but PRAYERS never will!

" A king who has no kingly power; how can he know what a king with kingly instincts enjoy?

Can darkness embrace the Sun ?

That which is not space, how can it understand what space is ?

And how can a red berry match ornaments of jewels ?

Therefore he who has not become of My form, how can he know where I am ? "

Sant Dnyaneshwar

His Name

"
His name is the greatest treasure and
my pure heart always treasured it.

The Guru confers the name.

WITHOUT THE NAME One remains
a beggar. "

Guru Nanak

Ego

" Can you sneeze on your own ?

Can you yawn, cough or even relieve yourself volitionally ?

Can you be hungry or sleepy as and when you want ?

You don't get your ego mixed up when you eat, drink, sleep, yawn or sneeze !

Then, why do you add ego to your intellect when you create literature or compose a philosophical or political essay ? "

("The Master")

Prayer

" A flame lights up, you have an
enthusiastic push, a great fervour
and you express that in words that
must be spontaneous if they are to be
true. It must come from the heart,
straight, without passing through the
head. That is Prayer. "

**Mother
(Pondicherry)**

The Compassionate King

Once in Rajasthan, there lived a pious Rajah who was equally rich in pecunia and piety. He believed in the religion of good life and was very charitable in disposition, habitually disbursing a large part of his wealth in alms, clothes and food to the poor.

His pleasure palaces were four in number, each meant for a different season of the year, and in his official royal residence, five benign spirits, in the form of icons lived in five special alcoves situated in the main hall.

One day, the Rajah came across a wood cutter sitting on a pavement, with the saddest countenance that he had ever seen. Evening was on the verge of wearing the dark cloak of night. On enquiry, he found that unless the woodcutter could sell his pile of wood before dark, he would not be able to place even a morsel in the mouth of his five dependents at home. The Rajah impulsively gave him one thousand golden coins, enough to last him right through his old age, and purchased the pile of wood which was duly placed by his cook in the palace kitchen.

As soon as that was done, all the icons in the five alcoves suddenly started weeping for some inscrutable reason!

From then onwards, the Rajah accelerated the size and frequency of his charities, to the extent that a proclamation was issued to decree that anyone with unsold wares must not return to his home at dusk without selling them to the Rajah, who would purchase them at any price demanded.

People came to know about his peculiar form of the charity and started taking undue advantage of his goodness. But the Rajah, even then, remained firm in his resolve. Gardually, however, his wealth started dwindling away, his estates started yielding fewer and fewer produce for want of proper care. His servants started leaving him; and one by one, his palaces were put on sale; but his resolve to purchase unsold wares at any price remained undeterred!

To his great surprise, he found one day that four of the spirits had left four of the alcoves and that the fifth icon was also on the verge of leaving. The Rajah's eyes welled up with tears.

Just then, from the first, second, third and fourth alcoves - the deities of wealth, justice, knowledge and aesthetics (art) started speaking in wailing tunes, rebuking the Rajah that it was well nigh impossible for them to stay there because of the King's unjust and frivolous extravagance. The fifth deity of RITA (righteousness; truth) was on the verge of leaving and at that juncture spoke the Rajah: "I accept that my foolish whims knew no bounds; but I did all this only because of my righteous resolve that prompted me to keep my promise to help the helpless. You are TRUTH and Rightousness; and now you too are leaving me! When TRUTH leaves a person, he has nothing left to live for and should put, therefore, a quick end to his life!

Hearing this, RITA - the deity presiding over Rightousness did not make any further move to leave; and the icon of Rightousness stepped back into the alcove. One by one, all the other four icons reinstated themselves in their respective alcoves. It was RITA that brought all the other four - wealth, justice, knowledge and aesthetics back into the royal residence.

Live with Righteousness but Never be Self Righteous

"Didn't I tell you what will happen? Something was told by someone and it happened exactly as was told by that person! It is very annoying to the listener; because to the listener, the words have come out from a self-righteous person.

Do not give importance to the vain-glorious attitude of a self-righteous person. The quality is more important than the person who vainly practices that quality.

We can be righteous without becoming ourselves self-righteous. In becoming self-righteous, we ask others, "DID YOU SEE OR NOT - I WAS SO MUCH RIGHT!"

This is a self-asserting attitude which to a simple person is very very annoying! Our practice of something GOOD shall remain 'good' & 'righteous' by staying righteous only and without annoying anyone who observes it!

Reality

You are a very sagacious reader, a wise human being. You keep your Reality when it faces you so as to realise it in its true shape and form.

1) We are helpless in our childhood and at that time some people in their advanced age keep us with great care and therefore they are like our parents. They grow old and at that time we can not ignore them and If you can look after them - you are proving yourself true to the Reality.

2) There are some young people who think very many times to place their parents in their old age into "THE HOME FOR THE AGED". Does it behove you well? Suppose, in your young age, they had admitted you in the orphanage! What could have been your condition?

3) Reality is very painful! Where parents become guests of their children - there the

Lord God stays most unwillingly or there the Lord does not stay at all!

GLARING TRUTH

One who lovingly pets a dog with love, finds the dog very faithful. This is the same attitude shown to a person by the loving parents - Can't you show your love and faithfulness to people who showed you love with great humility ? What ails you? Don't you have the eyes to see unblemished love and affection from persons who are always to prove their love as parents?

There are hypocrites who make great noise about their own love and affection about their parents when they live separately. They go so far upto keeping the name of their home as "PITRU CHHAYA" or "MATRU-NIWAS"; but, they would not think right to stay even for some time with their loving parents. The son becomes veritably funny, when he becomes so very blind to the love and affection of his own mother; but he goes mad before the sensuality of his own wife who entices him.

A Lady with her Son

It was Prophet Muhammad's time of preservation of his piety and integrity. When saints and prophets pass off their words of wisdom to us they give us an unmistakably rich legacy which never can be destroyed!

Two things harm us a lot. One is our apathy to be in tune with nature and the other is to turn a deaf ear to the voice within and indulge in ignorant babbling like discussing religion and advising others.

Hazrat Nabi (Prophet) Muhammad was at that time, in great demand by the people. They flocked around him in large numbers. His blessings performed miracles. He was, therefore, their goal and final hope.

One day, a lady approached the Prophet accompanied by her son. The boy's body was full of bruises, boils and skin abrasions. Nabi looked at her at once. She was in tears. She was hardly able to speak. The Prophet made her sit down near him and asked her to calm down.

After some time, when interrogated, she said that her son, being extremely fond of dry dates, was eating them in huge quantity, causing harm to his body. Besides that, the boy could not resist climbing date-palms with spikes bristling from the trunk. These spikes caused cuts, abrasions and bruises that turned into septic wounds and boils. The mother was at her wit's end and could not see any way out of this impasse. Hearing about the efficacy of Nabi's 'duas' (blessings) and 'bandagi' (prayers), she had approached the prophet for his blessings to cause an aversion for dates in her son's mind.

The prophet sat in silence after she completed her story. He told the mother to come again after a fortnight with her son. The lady was greatly disappointed. She thought the prophet would immediately accede to her small request and cure her son with the blessings. She returned home that day, crestfallen!

After fifteen days, immediately on approaching the prophet, the lady's wishes were fulfilled. The boy was blessed and the mother was assured that in future, her son would never touch dates again.

The mother gratefully rose; uttered her thanks and took her leave. As she was on the verge of crossing the front gate, she suddenly turned around and returned to the Prophet.

The Prophet asked her the reason for her unexpected return. She told the Nabi that she was curious about knowing the reason why he had not showered his blessings on the FIRST DAY itself, and why she had been called again after fifteen days. The Prophet paused for a moment. Then, he disclosed to her that he himself preferred dates as his food at all three meal-times of the day; and so he first wanted to test his non restraint and see whether he could himself give up (leave) dates totally (for ever) before he too prayed for the boy to give them up.

It was not that easy to pray for the boy unless he could not leave the dates for ever and totally; because dates had become a part and parcel of his food by now! Unless he abandons dates, he cannot ask someone to abandon them and that too totally!

A Sufi Mystic

Drunk without wine,
Sated without food,
Foodless and sleepless,
A king beneath a humble cloak,
A treasure within a ruin,
Not of air and earth,
Not of fire and water,
A sea within bounds.
He has a hundred moons and skies and suns.
He is wise through universal truths,
Not a scholar from a book.

Rumi

The Name

"

Some build palaces,

Others build thatched huts,

But even palaces vanish,

Listen, when you came here

You had no companions;

When you go, there will be none;

What use are the elephants housed
in your stables?

Kabir says that in the end you will go,

Like the gambler who has lost empty handed,

Unless you remember the

Name of the Lord. "

Kabir

Water

"   Of all the elements, the sage should take Water as his PRECEPTOR.

Water is yielding but all Conquering. Water extinguishes fire or finding itself defeated escapes as steam and reforms.

Water washes away soft earth or when confronted by rocks, seeks a way round.

Water corrodes iron till it crumples to dust. It saturates the atmosphere so that the wind dies. Water gives way to obstacles with deceptive humility; for, no power can prevent it following its destined course to sea.

Water conquers by yielding; it never attacks but always wins the last battle.

The sage who makes himself as water is distinguished for his humility; he embraces passivity, acts for non action and conquers the world! "

TAO YEN of NAN YEN
(11th century TAOIST Mystic)

A Prayer from the Bible

"Our father who art in Heaven!

Hallowed be Thy name!
Thy Kingdom come!

Thy will be done on earth, as it is in Heaven!

Give us this day, our daily bread, and forgive us our trespasses,

As we forgive them that trespass against us,

And allow us not to fall into temptation, but deliver us from evil!

For Thine is the Kingdom and the Power and the Glory for ever and ever!"

Amen!

Work

The word WORK is a coinage of the Devil! 'Work' that can help, that can activate some one to establish good, righteous and even nice should not be or can not be the coinage of the 'Devil'. It should be the coinage of an 'angel'.

Work and it is "GOOD WORK"

(Types and Types of Work)

'Work' can be labelled "HARD WORK'. Whether the work that takes more time can be termed as hard work and whether it can be termed GOOD WORK!

Work - that can make the person who has to experience the effects of the WORK most righteous or 'best' can be labelled "GOOD WORK".

Someone who works day and night and his

WORK - which could be very hard and devours more time! could that be good work? Possibly NOT. Some person who has to lower down or to connive at the quality of the WORK that he performs could not be labelled 'GOOD WORK'.

'GOOD' is always an adjective that means 'good' or 'righteous' only! It can be a preceding word that makes the reader well satisfied about the quality - the good or the best quality of the WORK that has been completed OR performed as BEST only.

Our Most Important Work

There are types and types of work and the most important work for us is to know our 'SELF' without any fear or favour. When we start knowing ourselves VERY DEEPLY we have started to know the 'SELF' sincerely!

Are we working on the strata of this earth aimlessly? Or are we doing so meaningfully? This meaning does not touch a shade of POLITICS, SCIENCE, OR ANY POWER - psychological or physical!

Am I considering myself a CITIZEN OF THE WORLD or NOT! Or DO I take myself as an Indian, or a French or a German? Even further a Parsee or a Parisian or a person belonging to the old Tutonic cult?

As long as we do not make it clear to ourselves that more we become free and simple to understand LIFE, more we become an understanding 'human being'! Therefore the most important WORK is definitely to convince us that we come here and survive WITH A PURPOSE.

Poorer than a Beggar

Swami Anand Swarup is in the habit of going fast into the SAHAJ SAMADHI (सहज समाधी). This great Yogi early every morning will go deep into Samadhi after he will sit in Padmyasan. His Yoga-Samadhi will not get disturbed. His Yoga Samadhi will remain unbroken.

One day a rich man came to see the Swamiji. Swamiji stood silently at the time of this meeting. "Tell me, if you have come to ask me any question", Swamiji asked the rich Shethji. "No, Swamiji, I have come to you to give something and not to receive any solution to my religious questions! I am blessed by God as regards the wealth; and I have come to give you one thousand Gold Mohurs with a request to you to use in social welfare!... an activity of your choice". Swami Anand Swarup closed the eyes as well as his mouth! and asked him; "You must be possessing abundant wealth and yet you are constantly endeavoring to acquire further and further wealth". To this, came the Shethji's reply in the affirmative. Therefore, you are still very poor and endeavoring to acquire further wealth. Such persons are poorer than beggars! It was the apt reply to Shethji.

A Living Friend of the Almighty, KABEER

You must be knowing our Noble Laureate Rabindranath Tagore who veritably drank the nectar poured out by Kabeer in his poems. Tagore, it was, who was most attracted by Kabeer's 'Dûhā' 'Awalwani', 'Bijak'. Tagore's first book of poems in English was named "POEMS OF KABEER".

The word "Kabeer" has come from the Arabic language and means - 'GREAT'; 'MIGHTY'. Other similar words indicating the same meaning are 'AKBAR'; 'AKĀBAR' etc. Kabeer's greatness is in his humble and plain thoughts, and in the directness of the language. His greatness is concerned in the simplicity of his greatness.

The Kabeer literally talks with you. To fathom Kabeer is to fathom an ocean. Kabeer doesn't like anybody being deceived. He says, "O

Kabeer, you may be deceived but never deceive anyone. Be happy in the knowledge that someone deceived you; for, you will be miserable in the constant thought that you have deceived some one!"

Kabeer is considered "a Living Saint". He pulsates in the veins of all true philosophers and all great poets like Rabindranath Tagore.

He says, My SAI- 'Master' is a Bania - Vepari, a Vanik businessman. His way of doing business is so natural and so different. He weighs all the actions of the people of this world. His weighing scale has neither the Centre - Rod nor the two plates hanging below and yet he weighs the whole SAMSĀRA - mundane world.

The Spiritual Master Punished a Prince

The follwing story is taken from the page of Iranian history some 7000 years ago. In and all around Iran, the name of the Emperor was uttered with great reverence. Prince Noshirwan was entrusted by his royal father to the spiritual Master, Iran's Vazir - Buzargchameher (बूझर्गचमेहेर) for his training.

He gave all the training that Prince Noshirwan was supposed to take. Riding, Fencing, Archery, etc. on the Martial training side and Law, Administration & human relations on the Mental Faculty side.

Both Noshirwan and Buzargchameher worked in harmony. Noshirwan was very grateful to his Master Trainer and almost a year elapsed in this benevolent GIVE AND TAKE.

One day, this, very righteous master came very near to Noshirwan and punished him with a stick without giving any reason for the punishment. In reality they were 2 strokes only.

Noshirwan was so obedient and good as a disciple that he could not, in any manner, accept the said punishment, because he was not ready for it!

He approached his father and asked him the reason why he was punished by the great Spiritual Master Buzargchameher without any rhyme or reason. The father and later also his mother felt very much inwardly but told him that they were helpless in bringing about any solution to the problem.

The time passed by and Noshirwan's father passed away. He felt very much alone and on top of it the Superiors of the Court discussed among themselves and fixed up a date for Coronation. As soon as the Coronation date was fixed, King Noshirwan now made himself bold to ask the great Master when he would come to place the Crown on his head in presence of the entire Assembly.

That day arrived. A great ceremony

consisting of 'Jashna' Prayers was performed and equally great Guru rose up to hold the crown which was to be placed on the head of King Noshirwan.

When the moment of placing the Crown on Noshirwan's head arrived, Noshirwan with great respect and boldness coupled with humility asked the Master to explain why he punished him some ten years back and coldly refused to give any explanation about why he was punished.

It was now the time for Vazir Buzargchameher not to keep quiet but to speak boldly about why he behaved in such a strange manner after the punishment was meted out to the King who was at that time - A Prince.

He said, "Sire ! I know that I am not fit for your mercy because of my mysterious behavior in not offering an explanation why you were punished without any rhyme or reason! Even after so many years, My lord you could not accept any unjust punishment and thus I wanted you to realise that when as a King you will not offter any unjust punishment to anyone great or small who has come to get justice in your court. If this what has happened comes to your mind and will goad you not to behave with your subjects in any strange manner".

"I pray my lord to forgive me to this lapse because I had to do it for the sake of getting your name in the list of Just and Noble Kings".

Following are some Anecdotes from the book
"One Minute Wisdom"
by Fr. Anthony de mello, S.J.

Identity

"How does one seek union with God?"

"The harder you seek, the more distance you create between Him and you."

"So what does one do about the distance?"

"Understand that it isn't there"

"Does that mean that God and I are one?"

"Not one. Not two."

"How is that possible?"

"The sun and its light, the ocean and the wave, the singer and his song - not one, not two."

Worship

"To the disciple who was overly respectful the Master said.

"Light is reflected on a wall.
Why venerate the wall?
Be attentive to the light.".

Discovery

"Help us to find God."

"No one can help you there."

"Why not?"

"For the same reason that no one can help the fish to find the ocean."

Expression

"He was a religious writer and interested in the Master's views. "How does one discover God?"

Said the Master sharply, "Through making the heart white with silent meditation, not making paper black with religious composition."

And, turning to his scholarly disciples, he teasingly added. "Or making the air thick with learned conversation."

Emptiness

"Sometimes there would be a rush of
noisy visitors and the silence of the
monastery would be shattered.

This would upset the disciples; not
the Master who seemed just as content
with the noise as with the silence.

To his protesting disciples he said
one day, "Silence is not the absence of
sound, but the absence of self.""

Innocence

"When out on a picnic the Master said:

"Do you want to know what the enlightened life is like? Look at those birds flying over the lake."

While everyone watched, the Master exclaimed:

"They cast a reflection on the water that they have no awareness of - and the lake has no attachment to."

Myths

"The Master gave his teaching in parables and stories which his disciples listened to with pleasure - and occasional frustration, for they longed for something deeper.

The Master was unmoved. To all their objections he would say. "You have yet to understand, my dears, that the shortest distance between a human being and Truth is a story."

Another time he said, "Do not despise the story. A lost gold coin is found by means of a penny candle; the deepest truth is found by means of a simple story."

Solitude

"I want to be with God in prayer."

"What you want is an absurdity."

"Why?"

"Because whenever you are, God is
not: Whenever God is, you are not.
So how could you be with God?"

Later the Master said:

"Seek aloneness. When you are with
someone else you are not alone. When
you are 'with God' you are not alone.
The only way to really be with God is to
be utterly alone. Then, hopefully,
God will be and you will not."

Repression

"The Master had been on his deathbed in a coma for weeks. One day he suddenly opened his eyes to find his favourite disciple there.

"You never leave my bedside, do you?" he said softly.

"No, Master. I cannot."'

"Why?"

"Because you are the light of my life."

The Master sighed. "Have I so dazzled you, my son, that you still refuse to see the light in you?"

Heaven

"To a disciple who was obsessed with the thought of life after death, the Master said, "Why waste a single moment thinking of the hereafter?"

"But is it possible not to?"

"Yes."

"How?"

"By living in heaven here and now."

"And where is this heaven?"

"It is here and now."

Words

"The disciples were absorbed in a discussion of Lao Tzu's dictum:

"Those who know do not say:

Those who say do not know."

When the Master entered they asked him exactly what the words meant.

Said the Master, "Which of you knows the fragrance of a rose?"

All of them knew.

Then he said, "Put it into words".

All of them were silent."

Credits

Thanks to those who took genuine interest in all my righteous endeavours to publish a book.

They are :

- My wife Navaaz.
- My daughter Mahrukh.
- My grandson Behzad, his wife Rhea and his son Yohaan.
- My publisher SOHIN LAKHANI.
- My well-wishers and friends who are eagerly awaiting this publication.
- Salim and Sabiha Sayed.
- Architect Hafeez Contractor & Mr. Eruch Chinwala.
- Kekobad Mehta & Boman Mehta (Darashaw).
- Mr. Neville K. P. Mehta - Managing Trustee of my school - Boy's Town Public School.
- Amongst them, one name is Shantiben Shah who helped me a lot by encouraging me to go through various books of similar philosophy.
- Shilpa is another similar name who tops the list of my inspirers.

www.ingramcontent.com/pod-product-compliance
Lightning Source LLC
Chambersburg PA
CBHW030527260626
47157CB00005B/1904